ISBN 978-0-35-868360-5 HC
ISBN 978-0-35-868361-2 PA

Typography by Stephanie Hays
22 23 24 25 26 LB 10 9 8 7 6 5 4 3 2 1   First Edition

I Can Read!

1 BEGINNING READING

PRETZEL AND THE PUPPIES

MEET THE PUPS!

Margret and H. A. Rey

CLARION BOOKS

An Imprint of HarperCollins *Publishers*

This is Pretzel.

He is a very long dog.

And these are his puppies:

Puck, Pippa, Pedro, Paxton, and Poppy.

They play games and solve problems.

They have a lot of fun together!

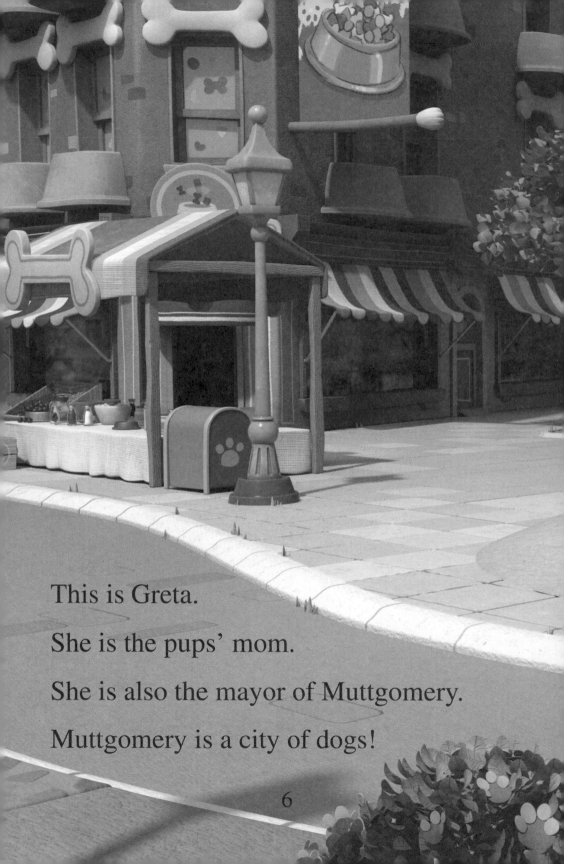

This is Greta.

She is the pups' mom.

She is also the mayor of Muttgomery.

Muttgomery is a city of dogs!

Puck, Paxton, Pedro, Pippa, and Poppy
make a great team.

Paxton is an artist.

He loves to draw and paint.

When he sees something beautiful

he has to draw it!

Poppy is a leader.

She reads a lot of books.

She is full of great ideas.

Nothing stops her!

Puck is funny.

He tells great jokes.

He likes to make his family laugh.

Dogs always smile when he is around.

Pippa is a performer.

She is a singer and a dancer.

She loves to get dressed up.

Fancy is fun!

Pedro is an athlete.

He may be small, but he is strong!

He loves to fetch and run.

He never gives up.

The pups love their city.

They love to help their neighbors.

Living in Muttgomery is the best!

They want to celebrate Muttgomery with their friends.

But how? They need a plan.

Time to get your paws up, pups!

21

The pups decide to have a parade.

They gather all they need.

Pedro will ride his scooter.

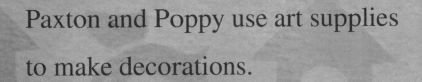

Paxton and Poppy use art supplies
to make decorations.

Pippa and Puck find costumes.

The pups are ready!

The puppy parade is off!

But a parade needs lots of dogs.

How will the pups make their parade

big enough to celebrate Muttgomery?

The pups can solve this problem.

Get your paws up, pups!

They spread the word.

Every dog in town will join in!

The dogs of Muttgomery

make a long parade.

They walk, roll, and sing songs.

They have fun being together.

Great job, pups.

You made a difference today.

You made your bark!

They walk, roll, and sing songs.

Thcy have fun being together.

Great job, pups.

You made a difference today.

You made your bark!